Archie and The Bluebs

Chapters

To Glenn,

A small token of my gratitude of your kind support.

Chapter I
Off to Hickery!

Very best wishes

Val

(Valerie Spearpoint - Author)

28/10/20.

It was the school summer holidays and young Archie Smythe an inquisitive boy of 7 and three quarters years of age, with red spiky hair and freckles is today setting off to the sleepy zzzZ little village of Hickery in the depths of the English countryside.

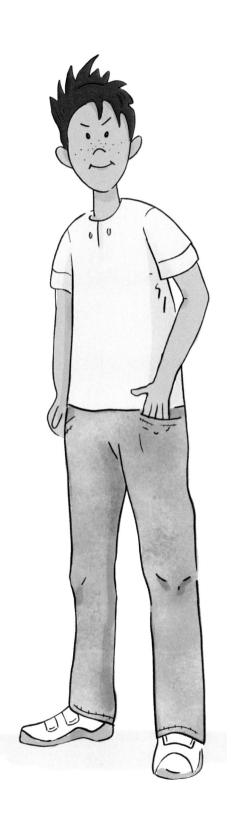

Archie is going to spend a week of his summer holidays with his Aunt Beth and Uncle Albert, both of whom he had never met.

His parents Fiona and Thomas are Antique Dealers and are off on a business trip for a week to Paris.

Fiona and Thomas's business trip unfortunately clashed with the school summer holidays and as there was no-one else available to look after Archie for the week they were away, Fiona contacted her Aunt Beth.

Fiona had also stayed with Aunt Beth and Uncle Albert when she was a teenager in the school summer holidays and they were always so kind to her and although Fiona had not seen Aunt Beth and Uncle Albert for many years, she had always kept in contact with them by post through exchange of cards and gifts.

"Come on Archie, time is ticking on and we have a long drive from London to your Aunt and Uncle's" said his Dad.

"Alright" said Archie.

Reluctantly, Archie picked up his suitcase and came down stairs and waited in the hall.

"Don't look so glum Archie, as I promise that you will really enjoy spending time with your Uncle and Aunt, and Aunt Beth bakes the best cakes ever.

Anyway, a week without technology at your fingertips will not do you any harm whatsoever" said Archie's Mum as she came into the hall.

"Archie you will be fine and it is only a week" said his Dad still trying to reassure him.

"Ok" said Archie, shrugging his shoulders….. wondering how he would cope with no internet access and no-one else his own age to hang out with.

Although, he did take some of his favourite books to read in case the boredom set in.

They all got in the car and set off for Hickery with gifts from London for Aunt Beth and Uncle Albert.

It was late afternoon before they finally arrived in Hickery, but to get to Aunt Beth and Uncle Albert's house they had to drive down a long country lane in the middle of nowhere.

They drove through a dark wood with trees over hanging the lane, making it look and feel very *SPOOOOOKY...*

As they got closer to the edge of the woods it started to get lighter as there were less and less trees.

When they came out of the woods Archie felt a sudden shiver.

"That felt strange" thought Archie.

"Here we are!" said Fiona, as they drove up the gravel drive to Aunt Beth and Uncle Albert's home.

They pulled up in front of a beautiful redbrick house with roses rambling up the side of the porch and lavenders growing in the borders under the windowsills.

Aunt Beth and Uncle Albert heard the car pull up outside and came out to greet them.

"Welcome, welcome! Fiona and Thomas. It's so wonderful to see you both after such a long time" said Uncle Albert.

"This must be Archie! We have heard so much about you from your parents and how lovely it is to have you spend time with us this summer. You are the image of your father, but you do have your mothers' big beautiful curious brown eyes" said Aunt Beth.

Archie didn't know what to say to his Aunt Beth and just went bright PINK with embarrassment and said a polite "Thank you".

Fiona ran over to her Aunt and Uncle and gave them a big hug.

"Come on in then Archie, I have some homemade fruit cake and I will put a pot of tea on for us all" said Aunt Beth.

Aunt Beth and Uncle Albert were in their early 70's.

Aunt Beth had soft grey hair tied up in a bun and she still had her apron tied around her waist covered in flour from the kitchen, where she had been baking cakes that afternoon.

Uncle Albert had curly white hair and a curly white beard to match and you could tell from his belly that he had been eating a lot of Aunt Beth's cakes as he looked quite FULL........

It was like stepping back in time when Archie walked into the house, as it was full of antique furniture and there was a very old tall Grandfather clock that stood out in the hallway.

The idea of homemade fruit cake sounded great to Archie and if this is the start of things to come for the week, it was a good start as he loved ♥ CAKE.

The family had tea and cake and Uncle Albert showed Archie to his huge bedroom at the top of the house where he would sleep for the next week.

"Make yourself at home Archie as we want you to enjoy your stay with us" said Uncle Albert.

"Thank you Uncle Albert" said Archie.

Archie unpacked his suitcase and put his belongings away.

"Well, I am here now and Aunt Beth and Uncle Albert seem very nice" Archie thought to himself.

It was soon early evening after a late afternoon tea and a lovely catch up for Fiona with her Aunt and Uncle after quite a few years.

It was also time for Fiona and Thomas to return to London and set off on their business trip.

"We are off now Archie" his parents shouted upstairs.

Archie ran downstairs and hugged his parents. They all said their goodbyes and he waved his parents off at the front door with Aunt Beth and Uncle Albert.

"It is time for a bath and bed now Archie" said Aunt Beth.

Archie had his bath, put his pyjamas on ready for bed and came downstairs to say goodnight to Aunt Beth and Uncle Albert.

"Goodnight" said Aunt Beth and Uncle Albert.

As Archie walked back through the hallway before climbing the staircase to his bedroom, he looked at the Grandfather clock and noticed that it had softly painted Bluebells on the clock face that looked almost real.

Archie then went off up the wooden staircase to bed.

Archie lay in bed wondering how the next week would be in Hickery with Aunt Beth and Uncle Albert, as there was no mobile phone signal, they had no internet so he could not play any online games, no-one else his own age to hang out with etc etc etc....and then finally...., he fell asleep kicking out the ZZZZ.

Chapter II
Meet The Bluebs!

It was just before 11 o'clock at night and suddenly Archie woke up as he could hear someone talking quietly on the landing outside his bedroom.

"Who is that?" he thought.

He could hear Aunt Beth and Uncle Albert *SNOOOOORING* in the bedroom below him so it definitely wasn't them.

Then he heard what sounded like tiny footsteps running down the stairs.

Archie lay in bed thinking "should I get up and have a look or just pretend that I didn't hear anything??????".

CURIOSITY got the better of him being a *CURIOUS BOY* and he quickly got up, put his dressing gown and slippers on, grabbed the torch off the bedside cabinet and slowly opened his bedroom door.

A slow *CREEEEEEK....* could be heard as he opened the door.

Archie came out of his bedroom and crept down the stairs shining his torch on the stairs as he went.

He got to the bottom stair and then suddenly he saw the door of the Grandfather clock open and shut quickly.

"That is really odd......" thought Archie.

He walked up to the Grandfather clock and slowly opened the door wondering what he might find…….

What he saw was in fact an old wooden lift inside.

"Am I dreaming?" Archie thought and then shone his torch inside and saw a big button that said, "PRESS ME IF YOUR DARE!!!".

Archie thought "shall I DARE get in the lift? or shan't I?" and being a CURIOUS BOY HE DID! and squeezed himself through the door and in to the lift.

As soon as he was in the lift he felt strangely odd, as although he had to squeeze through the door there was suddenly lots of room and the lift was HUGE!.....inside.

Archie shut the door and decided that he would DARE!!! to press the button!......BRAVE or CURIOUS BOY DO YOU THINK!? BOTH I SAY!!

"Here I go!" said Archie as he pressed the button!

The lift SHOT OFF!!

"AAAAAAH!" screamed Archie as the lift shot off downwards so fast, he grabbed on to the handrail in the lift and held on tight.

The LIFT SWERVED LEFT and *RIGHT* and *RIGHT* and LEFT...and then eventually stopped with a.... THUD!!!

DING!! the door opened into a VERY DARK SPOOKY! wood.

Archie peeled himself off the handrail after holding on so tight.... and then shone his torch into the dark.

He could see silhouettes of what looked like huge dead trees with no leaves on and their branches were hanging so heavily they looked VERY VERY SAD ☹ ...

Suddenly! two little creatures appeared in front of the lift door!

They both had quiffed hair and blue faces. One had blue quiffed hair and the other red quiffed hair.

They had twigs for arms and twigs for legs and they were dressed in red striped blue tartan trousers and waistcoats, with braces and they were wearing red hobnail boots.

"AAAAAAAH!" screamed Archie again.

"HUSH!" said the creature with the blue quiffed hair "as you will alert the MYSTERIOUS DARKNESS".

"Quick follow us as we need to hide you!" the little creatures said.

"Who are you and what are you???!!" said Archie.

"I am Dougie and this is Trevor and we are the BLUEBS" said Dougie with the blue quiffed hair.

"We are the keepers of the wood and we need to hide you quickly to keep you safe!!" said Trevor with the red quiffed hair.

There was clearly no time to wait! so Archie got out of the lift and ran behind Dougie and Trevor in the darkness shining his torch as he ran.

"Where are we going???" said Archie.

"Somewhere safe from the MYSTERIOUS DARKNESS!" said Dougie.

They stopped in front of a huge dark oak tree and Dougie turned a notch on the tree and a door opened.

"Quick get in!" said Trevor.

The tree door slammed shut behind them and suddenly there was light.

"WOW this tree is HUGE!" said Archie.

"Welcome to BLUEB HQ" said Dougie.

Archie looked up and the inside of the tree was adorned in light from the fairy lights attached to the wooden staircase, as it spiralled all the way up to the top of the inside of the tree through wooden floors.

On each floor he could see what looked like lots and lots of hessian sacks tied up with string and they looked very heavy.

On the ground floor where he was stood there were wooden bunkbeds, a rickety old kitchen, a kettle that was whistling away over an open fire and a wooden table with chairs to sit on.

"Trevor, the kettle is about to boil please can you make us all a mug of tea" said Dougie.

"This is no ordinary oak tree Archie and although it does look and feel like the inside of a wooden tree house it is actually made of a very strong precious metal and is hiding our spaceship below" said Dougie.

"That is AMAZING!!" said Archie.

"Yes, it sure is" said Trevor as he was pouring the tea.

"I have just realised" said Archie.

"realised what?" said Dougie.

"I have SHRUNK and I am now only 6 INCHES TALL!!! what has happened to me????" said Archie.

"Hey, what are you worrying about Archie? Chill out, you are in a different world now and that is why" said Dougie.

"How do you know my name as I haven't told you??" said Archie.

"Archie, we knew of you already and we were in your Aunt and Uncle's house when you arrived. Where do you think the fairy lights, tea bags, cake and everything else has come from?" said Dougie.

"My Aunt and Uncle's house?" said Archie.

"Yes, your Aunt and Uncle have so much stuff In their house that they have not missed anything and your Aunt bakes so many cakes (great cakes by the way!) that they will never eat them all, so we help them out by eating cake too" said Dougie.

"Sit down Archie and have a mug of tea and I will explain" said Trevor.

"The only way to get to your Aunt and Uncle's house is through the wood that you drove through today with your parents and that wood is where you are now.

Tonight, you have come through a doorway from one world and into another.

This wood was a beautiful Bluebell wood. The trees stood tall and proud and the sun shone its streams of light through the wood on to the Bluebells showing them in all their glory, as a beautiful blanket of blue wild flowers trailing through the wood.

Bees could be seen BUZZING around happily from one Bluebell to another keeping them safe.

NOW!.....the MYSTERIOUS DARKNESS is here....and the Bluebells and the Bees are hiding, as bit by bit the MYSTERIOUS DARKNESS is pulling everything else into its darkness FOREVER!" said Trevor.

"This is like a bad dream?" said Archie

"Absolutely!" said Trevor.

"Where has the MYSTERIOUS DARKNESS come from, what is it and why is it here?" said Archie.

"The MYSTERIOUS DARKNESS is from a MYSTERIOUS PLANET and is a cold dark shadow that lives and hides in the shadows from light.

Its own planet was destroyed by the GOOD LIGHT to stop the darkness from spreading to other planets, but the MYSTERIOUS DARKNESS escaped to earth to find a place to hide and landed in this wood.

It wants to spread its darkness, taking over the earth and turning it into total darkness so it can live forever and everything else will be destroyed as there will be no LIGHT!

The doorway to this world is a magical one, through the Grandfather clock in your Aunt and Uncle's house and this doorway has been here for a 1000 years.

The doorway was made to look like a Grandfather clock by a very clever, wise, kind and wonderful wizard by the name of Zenry Augustus, or Bob as he prefers to be called for short.

Bob could see into the future and knew that one day the MYSTERIOUS DARKNESS would come to earth.

We have been sent from our PLANET BLUEB by the GOOD LIGHT and we are the keepers of the wood in the future. The GOOD LIGHT was also created by Bob to help you. We have been waiting for the moment, when one day you would come to this wood.

As Bob foretold over a 1000 years ago, you were the one
that would be chosen to come to this wood and save the wood and
the earth from the MYSTERIOUS DARKNESS!" said Trevor.

"WOW! this is unbelievable! When can I start?" said Archie.

After going from "scared Archie" to "fearless Archie saviour
of the earth" was such a quick change, that Trevor and
Dougie just looked at each other speechless and opened
mouthed.....

"Now might be a good time??!!!" said Trevor.

"Right then! Let's make a plan" said Archie.

"I will find paper, pens and sticky tape from my Aunt and Uncle's
house, to help us map out a battle plan at BLUEB HQ.

We can destroy the MYSTERIOUS DARKNESS FOREVER!" said
Archie.

"Oh..... and how can I tell the difference between the normal
darkness in the wood and the MYSTERIOUS DARKNESS????"
said Archie.

"The MYSTERIOUS DARKNESS is of no being. It is a dark figure
with a pointed face and a pointed nose, poking out of a dark
hooded cloak with long sleeves that drape down showing its long
bony hands and fingers. It moves secretly through the woods in the
breeze of the shadows.

Before it gets near, you will suddenly feel an ice cold breeze coming towards you and then hear whispers calling you in to the darkness.

The whispers will get louder and louder as it tries to draw you in and you MUST ignore the WHISPERS! as suddenly before you know it, its huge cloak will wrap around you and you will feel yourself being pulled into a BLACK HOLE OF DARKNESS FOREVER!" said Trevor.

"OMG!! I don't like the sound of that at all!" said Archie.

"It is a lot to take in I know Archie, but we need to think about getting you back to the lift safely before the morning and before your Aunt and Uncle are awake!" said Dougie.

"I never thought about how to get back, with all this excitement as it doesn't seem real!" said Archie.

"It most certainly is real, as real as the freckles on your face and my blue hair!" said Dougie.

"So how do I get back here tomorrow night?" said Archie.

"Wait until it is 11 o'clock at night and your Aunt and Uncle are asleep and do exactly what you did tonight and get in the lift through the Grandfather clock, press the button and away you go. We will hide in the undergrowth near the lift and wait for you to arrive" said Dougie.

"Right then! Are you ready Archie?" said Trevor.

"As when we open the door, you will have to run as fast as you can behind us to the lift. Don't look back, just focus on where you are going and close your mind to anything else around you. If the MYSTERIOUS DARKNESS knows that you are thinking about it, then you will start to feel the ice cold breeze coming towards you!" said Trevor.

"Ok I will. When I return, I will bring back what we need to start our battle plan at BLUEB HQ" said Archie.

"Bring some homemade cake too!!!!" said Dougie.

"Will do!" said Archie.

"Here we go!" said Dougie.

Dougie opened the door of BLUEB HQ and said "Let's go!"

Dougie ran out of the door as fast as his hobnail boots would carry him with Trevor and Archie in hot pursuit behind him and Archie was shining his torch in the dark as they ran.

They were just coming up to the lift when suddenly Archie stumbled and fell over a small log as he lost his concentration and then suddenly from the shadows.....

"Archie, Archie...." Whispered the MYSTERIOUS DARKNESS.

Archie could hear the whispering in the distance calling him and as the whispers were getting louder and louder, the wind in the trees was getting stronger and stronger very quickly and blowing a gale.

Dougie helped Archie get up and held on tight to Archie as they approached the lift, to stop Archie from being pulled in to the darkness by the MYSTERIOUS DARKNESS!

"Follow my voice Archie, follow me...." whispered the MYSTERIOUS DARKNESS through the wind.

"Oh no!" said Archie.

"Hold on Archie!" said Dougie.

"I am trying, but I am getting very cold and I can feel myself being pulled away as I can't stand up properly! The wind is so strong!" said Archie.

"Archie, Archie can you hear me.....I am going to destroy you!" bellowed the MYSTERIOUS DARKNESS.

"Ha ha ha ha ha!!!!" screamed the MYSTERIOUS DARKNESS.

Trevor pushed against the strong wind to open the lift door.

"Hold on Archie!!" said Trevor.

Trevor pulled the lift door open with all his might and Trevor and Dougie both pushed Archie in to the lift and pushed the door shut!

Archie hit the lift button and as it SHOT OFF! he could feel the strength of the wind outside banging on the lift trying to get in!

As soon as the lift shot off Dougie and Trevor ran against the wind in their big hobnail boots back to BLUEB HQ.....and the MYSTERIOUS DARKNESS retreated in to the shadows as Archie had gone.

The first attempt by the MYSTERIOUS DARKNESS to trap Archie had failed!...Thankfully!!!

"Get in!" shouted Trevor to Dougie as he opened the oak tree door.

The door shut tight!!!!

"That was a close shave!" said Trevor.

"Too close! I need a cup of tea, put the kettle on" said Dougie.

Meanwhile….. the lift had just stopped with a THUD! inside the Grandfather clock in the hallway of Aunt Beth and Uncle Albert's home.

"Phew! That was unbelievable and very scary!" said Archie to himself.

He slowly opened the Grandfather clock door and this time it seemed much easier to get out than when he got in earlier that night, he thought.

He crept upstairs shining his torch on each stair and thankfully he could still hear Aunt Beth and Uncle Albert SNOOORING away as he passed their bedroom door on the way back up to his.

He switched his torch off and put it back where he found it, took his slippers and dressing gown off and got in to bed.

"What a night!!" he thought and fell asleep.

Chapter III
The Next Day!

It was 9am when Archie eventually woke up and he woke up to the sound of Aunt Beth walking into his bedroom and the smell of hot toast. Aunt Beth brought in a mug of tea and marmalade on toast on a tray for Archie's breakfast.

"Wakey wakey Archie! time to get up now as you don't want to miss the beautiful sunshine today!" said Aunt Beth.

"Thank you, Aunt Beth for breakfast. I love marmalade on toast it is one of my favourites" said Archie.

"Yes I know, as it was one of your Mum's favourites too when she was young" said Aunt Beth.

Archie enjoyed his breakfast and got himself ready for the day and his mission to find all the items he needed so that he, Dougie and Trevor could start putting together their battle plan to defeat the MYSTERIOUS DARKNESS!

Archie came downstairs and his Uncle and Aunt were in the lounge listening to the radio.

"What would you like to do today Archie?" said Aunt Beth.

"We are going to do some gardening, pick some strawberries and enjoy the sunshine. Would you like to join us Archie?" said Uncle Albert.

"Thank you, I would like to help and especially help you pick some Strawberries…!" said Archie.

"Eat as many strawberries as you want Archie as there are far too many for us" said Uncle Albert.

"Sounds great!" said Archie.

Archie had a lovely morning helping his Uncle and Aunt and eating plenty of strawberries, but he needed to find an excuse so that he could start getting everything ready for his journey back to the woods that night.

It was midday and Archie asked his Aunt Beth if he could go back to the house. He used the excuse that he had brought some of his favourite books with him that he wanted to start reading.

"Aunt Beth, I am full of strawberries now and would you mind if I went back to the house? as I have some books I would like to start reading" said Archie.

"Yes of course you can Archie" said Aunt Beth.

"We will be back in about an hour and I will make a lovely lunch for us all, with homemade scones, fresh cream and more strawberries for afternoon tea later" said Aunt Beth.

"Thank you" said Archie.

Archie got back to the house and started his mission to find paper, pens, sticky tape, paper clips and of course the much requested (CAKE!) and put it all in his rucksack under his bed ready for that night......DONE!

He jumped up on to his bed and got one of his favourite books out to enjoy some reading, but after 10 minutes of reading he drifted.... off to sleep.

"Archie, lunch is ready!" shouted Aunt Beth upstairs to Archie.

FOOD! Archie's eyes opened wide and he jumped up and ran downstairs.

He had a lovely lunch of cheese and potato pie with vegetables fresh from the garden and then an afternoon tea of homemade scones, fresh cream and strawberries just as Aunt Beth had promised.

Archie was feeling very content and FULL of lots of lovely food. DELICIOUS!

It was early evening before Archie knew it and time for his bath and bed.

As he always did with his parents, he came downstairs to say good night to his Aunt and Uncle.

"Good night" said Aunt Beth and Uncle Albert and they gave Archie a hug goodnight.

"Thank you for a lovely day" said Archie and off he went up the wooden staircase to bed.

Archie set his alarm clock to go off 15 minutes before 11 o'clock at night.

He had to give himself enough time to get ready and get downstairs to the lift in the Grandfather clock and head off back to the woods for his MISSION.

Chapter IV
Showdown!

Suddenly, Archie's bedroom door burst open and his bedroom filled with light!

Stood in the doorway was a little man. He had spectacles perched on the end of his nose, blue spiky hair, a blue curly beard and was dressed in a blue suit with a gold tie.

Over the top of his suit he was wearing a Mod Parka style coat with rainbow coloured buttons and he was carrying a rainbow coloured umbrella. His shoes were gold winklepickers that curled up at the toes.

"What's that!!" shouted Archie as he woke up startled by the light.

"Shhhh Archie, you will wake your Aunt and Uncle" said the little Man...very softly.

"Who are you?" said Archie hesitantly.

"I am Zenry Augustus the Wizard, or Bob for short if you prefer" said Bob.

Archie looked stunned as the wizard that Dougie and Trevor had been talking about was actually there in front of his eyes.

"You are the wizard that created the MAGICAL DOORWAY to the woods!" said Archie.

"That's right Archie" said Bob.

"Why are you here?" said Archie.

"I have been watching from afar in the past and I can see the MYSTERIOUS DARKNESS getting stronger and stronger very quickly and much quicker than I expected" said Bob.

"OMG!" said Archie.

"Look out of your bedroom window into the night and you will see that everything outside is starting to disappear and being pulled into a huge black swirling hole in the sky!" said Bob.

Archie looked out of his bedroom window and he could see the huge black hole in the dark sky swirling round and round, getting closer and closer to Aunt Beth and Uncle Albert's house.

"That looks really scary!" said Archie.

Suddenly, the house started to shake, the furniture in his bedroom started to move and the lights were flickering.

However! still Aunt Beth and Uncle Albert could be heard SNOOOOORING!!! away in their bedroom below!!!

"What is happening??" said Archie.

"Quick there is no time to waste!!!" said Bob.

Archie put his dressing gown and slippers on, grabbed his rucksack from under his bed and Bob said "Are you ready?"

"Yes, I think?!" said Archie.

They ran to the staircase to get downstairs to the Grandfather clock, but as they got to the staircase it started to sway and one by one each stair vanished in to thin air leaving gaping holes in the staircase.

"Look!" said Archie.

Suddenly, icy hands were crawling their way up the staircase turning everything in its path to ice!

"It's the MYSTERIOUS DARKNESS!!" shouted Bob.

"I am freezing and I can't feel my hands!" said Archie as he started to shiver.

"What shall we do!" shouted Archie to Bob.

"This!" said Bob.

Bob pressed one of the rainbow coloured buttons on his Parka coat and suddenly they were stood in front of the Grandfather clock in the hallway.

"What just happened and how did we get here?" said Archie.

"It's good old fashioned MAGIC!" said Bob.

"Look around us! there is no floor other than what we and the Grandfather clock are stood on and it's icy cold!!" said Archie.

An icy wind started to bellow through the house and all Archie could see was the house and everything in it being pulled upwards through a huge hole in the roof and into the sky. It was like being stood on the edge of a cliff!

Furniture was flying around and walls were collapsing. The wind was freezing cold, sending chills through their bones.

"The MYSTERIOUS DARKNESS is trying to stop us from getting to the woods Archie!" said Bob.

Archie suddenly slipped on the icy floor and slid over the edge! but just managed to grab hold of Bob's umbrella before he slipped away forever through the huge black hole!

"I'm slipping! and can't hold on much longer as I am so cold!" said Archie.

"Hold on, hold on!" said Bob.

Archie was dangling in mid-air being blown around in the wind and Bob dug his heels into the icy floor and pulled Archie back up on to the floor edge.

"Now stand behind me Archie against the clock, away from the edge and don't move!" said Bob.

"Ok" said a very weary Archie.

"I need to use a little more MAGIC to stop time and to stop everything from being sucked into the huge black hole. It will give us a chance to get back to the woods, as we do not have days anymore to defeat the MYSTERIOUS DARKNESS, we now have one night, so tonight is it!" said Bob.

"OH NO!" said Archie.

"What about my Aunt and Uncle and my Mum and Dad?" said Archie.

"They will all be safe, as your Mum and Aunt are descendants of the Zames Robert Clan" said Bob.

"Uh?" said Archie.

"No time to explain Archie and we can discuss this later, as now we have to go!" said Bob.

Bob said the MAGIC word "SLLEBUELB!" pronounced "SLLEB-U-ELB" and everything around Archie became a complete blur of colour, like the distorted mirrors found at a funfair and everything suddenly stopped and was completely still.

"WOW!" said Archie.

"Quick, get in the lift!" said Bob.

Archie and Bob got into the lift, pressed the button and off they shot, but this time the lift was transparent and Archie could see the moon, the stars and other planets. It was spectacular!

"Is this real?! are we travelling through space!?" said Archie.

"Yes" said Bob.

"This is AWESOME!" said Archie as he gazed out of the lift at the wonders of space.

"The normal way through time travel has been blocked by the MYSTERIOUS DARKNESS! as it is trying to block every entrance to the woods" said Bob.

"Now hold on tight to the handrail Archie, as we are about to come down to earth very quickly with a THUD!" said Bob.

THUD! The lift hit the ground in the woods!

Dougie and Trevor were hiding in the undergrowth waiting for Archie to arrive, but they had no idea that Bob would be with him too.

The lift door opened and out ran Archie and then Bob.

Dougie and Trevor came up from the undergrowth and were gob smacked when they saw Bob with Archie.

"Quick Dougie and Trevor, come and stand by us!" said Bob.

"What's going on, what has brought you here Bob???" said Dougie.

"I will explain when we are safe at BLUEB HQ!" said Bob.

Dougie and Trevor ran over and stood beside Archie.

Bob said the MAGIC word "SLLEB-U-ELB create a TUNNEL OF LIGHT!" and suddenly they were all stood in a TUNNEL OF LIGHT.

"Quick Dougie and Trevor, take us to BLUEB HQ as the tunnel of light will not last long and it is protecting us from being found by the MYSTERIOUS DARKNESS!" said Bob.

As they ran towards BLUEB HQ the tunnel of light moved with them protecting them as they ran.

Dougie turned the notch on the oak tree to open the door and in they ran.

"So what has happened since yesterday?" said Trevor.

"The MYSTERIOUS DARKNESS was trying to stop Archie from getting to the woods!! so I had to come back. The MYSTERIOUS DARKNESS is getting stronger and more clever by the minute and any battle plan that you may have had will no longer defeat the MYSTERIOUS DARKNESS, as it is only MAGIC that will save the day now!" said Bob.

"We can't do MAGIC though" said Trevor.

"Archie can" said Bob.

"Me? How come?" said Archie.

"You are a descendant of the Zames Robert Clan who have lived in these Bluebell woods for centuries and who still are the protectors of the wood. In fact, they are still living in these woods in the past and it has to be protected for the future to exist.

Zames Robert himself is a wonderful man and there is also Zedward The Genius who does genius things and Zonald The Mischievous who is full of fun and mischief.

All of Zames Roberts' siblings are of a curious nature, but it was Zandra The Good who inherited mystical powers from their mother Beattie The Wise" said Bob.

"So, how come I can do MAGIC then?" said Archie.

"Since Zandra The Good, the last person to inherit her MYSTICAL POWERS was your Aunt Beth and now it has been passed on to you" said Bob.

"WOW!" said Archie, Dougie and Trevor together.

"Are you all ready?" said Bob.

"Yes, I guess so…" said Archie, Dougie and Trevor together again.

"Dougie, where are all the Bluebell bulbs?" said Bob.

"They are all in hessian sacks up above us in the tree" said Dougie.

"Great!" said Bob.

"So, what do we do now?" said Archie.

"You need to lure the MYSTERIOUS DARKNESS out of the Shadows" said Bob.

"How are we going to do that?" said Dougie.

"Archie is going to call on all the forces of nature using his MAGIC! and you are going to help him. I can't intervene at any time, as it is only the three of you together that can do this. If I intervene it will change the course of history and I must not do that!!" said Bob.

"Archie, take my Parka coat and put it on as it has MAGICAL POWERS and it will also strengthen your MAGIC. You will know how to use it instinctively" said Bob.

Archie put on Bob's Parka coat and suddenly there was a glow of light around him!

"Quick get our sunglasses!" said Dougie to Trevor.

"This is immense!" said Trevor.

Dougie and Trevor put their sunglasses on to protect their eyes from the glow.

"WOW! Suddenly I feel very strong" said Archie

"You are!" said Bob.

"It's time to face the MYSTERIOUS DARKNESS!" said Bob.

Bob opened the door of BLUEB HQ and out Archie stepped with Bob, Dougie and Trevor behind him.

Trevor and Dougie stood either side of Archie with their arms flexed ready to take on the MYSTERIOUS DARKNESS! and Bob stood to one side as he could not intervene.

"You can take your sunglasses off now Dougie and Trevor as it is dark out here" said Archie chuckling inwardly to himself.

"Oh yes, thanks" said Dougie and Trevor and took their sunglasses off.

"Go on then Archie" said Bob.

"MYSTERIOUS DARKNESS, I call upon you to show yourself!" said a very nervous, but very brave Archie.

Nothing happened! and they all looked at each other....

Then suddenly, the breeze started to move across the ground, the air became very cold and they could see their breath in the air of the dark night.

A deep scary voice then emerged from the darkness making the ground shake with every word.

"I am stronger than you! YOU have no power that can defeat me! Let me show you!"

Suddenly the ground started to open up creating huge crevasses, thunder and lightning filled the sky and a whirlwind was heading towards Archie, Bob, Dougie and Trevor, pulling up trees in its path!

Bob, Trevor and Dougie dug their heels in hard to the ground by Archie, trying to steady their balance as the wind bellowed at them.

"Is this the best you can DO?" said Archie trying to draw the MYSTERIOUS DARKNESS out of the shadows.

"Show yourself MYSTERIOUS DARKNESS!!! or will you always HIDE in the shadows?!!!" said Archie.

"I am not afraid of YOU!!!" said the MYSTERIOUS DARKNESS.

A HUGE BONY FACE suddenly appeared in front of Archie!

"BOO!" it said to Archie.

"AAAAAAAAAHHHHHHHHHHHH!!!!!" screamed Archie and jumped six feet high in the air!

Dougie and Trevor's faces went from blue to white and white to blue in colour and their hair went from slick quiffs to standing on end with shock…! as they ran up the side of a tree….

Bob stood firm and just glared at the MYSTERIOUS DARKNESS….

When Archie stopped screaming….he realised that he was still six feet up in the air and the MYSTERIOUS DARKNESS had disappeared.

"Bob! What's happened! I am stuck up in the air! Help me!" said Archie.

"Archie, you have the MAGIC and must now use it. The Parka coat will protect you! Use your MAGIC and the Parka coat!! Think like a descendant of the Zames Robert Clan!!!!! You can do it Archie!!!!!" said Bob.

"Trevor and Dougie, what are you doing up a tree???" said Archie.

"Just getting a little exercise...." they both said whilst hugging the tree very tightly, as the whirlwind was throwing everything around them in its path.......

"Mmmmmmm" said Archie.

Dougie and Trevor then promptly ran back down the tree very quickly…..and shouted up to Archie "How can we help Archie???"

"I need to send Bob back to BLUEB HQ quickly, as the MYSTERIOUS DARKNESS may try and tempt Bob in to using his powers to protect us and change the course of history. As Bob said, he cannot intervene" said Archie.

"Bob" said Archie.

"Yes Archie" said Bob.

"Open up your umbrella and jump in to it quickly" said Archie.

Bob pressed the button on his umbrella and it opened up in to a huge umbrella and he jumped in.

"There you go!" said Archie.

Archie clicked his fingers, the umbrella closed and Bob disappeared in a puff of smoke.

"Woosh…..!" was the sound of Bob flying down the staircase of BLUEB HQ in his umbrella stopping promptly at the bottom.

"That was fun! Well done Archie! Good chap!" said Bob to himself.

The umbrella opened up, Bob got out and the umbrella returned to its normal size.

"Time to put a brew on!" said Bob.

Meanwhile.......the whirlwind was getting closer, the thunder and lightning was getting stronger and Archie, Dougie and Trevor needed to move fast!

"Right then, here we go!!" said Archie.

"Here stand on these" said Archie to Dougie and Trevor.

Archie pulled two rainbow coloured buttons off the Parka coat and threw them to the ground in front of Dougie and Trevor. The buttons immediately turned in to brightly coloured surf boards.

"Quick, jump on the surf boards and join me up here" said Archie.

"Wow these are cool" said Dougie and Trevor.

They jumped on the surf boards and they flew up to Archie.

"This is very wobbly!" said Trevor trying to find his balance on his surf board in the wind.

"Don't worry you will get used to it!" said Archie.

"Here, catch these" said Archie.

Archie pulled off another two buttons from his Parka and threw one each to Dougie and Trevor.

This time the buttons turned in to gold encrusted Bluebell shields.

"Hold the shields in front of you as they are MAGIC and will protect you" said Archie.

"You take on the thunder and lightning and I will go after the whirlwind" said Archie.

"Let's do this!!" shouted Dougie and Trevor.

Dougie and Trevor flew through the air on their surf boards directly into the path of the lightning bolts, holding their shields proudly in front of them whizzing around dodging the falling branches and trees as they were being pulled up out of the ground by the wind.

Every time a lightning bolt hit their shields the lightning bounced back in to the darkness exploding like fireworks, lighting up the sky and drowning the noise of the thunder.

Trevor and Dougie were darting around like fire flies in the night, at super high speed.

Archie flew in to the top of the whirlwind and then straight down through the centre of it to the very bottom. He grabbed the whirlwind by it's tail and threw it up high in to the sky.

"Take that MYSTERIOUS DARKNESS!" shouted Archie.

The whirlwind hurtled through the sky and disappeared in to outer space, the thunder and lightning stopped and everything stood still.

"Just one to go now, the MYSTERIOUS DARKNESS itself!" said Archie.

"Well done, Trevor and Dougie! great job!" said Archie.

"Thanks Archie, that was exhausting, but amazing" said Dougie and Trevor.

Just when they thought they were safe.....a very loud stomping noise appeared from nowhere making the ground shake and as they looked up the MYSTERIOUS DARKNESS was towering over them.

Trevor gulped and said "Uh oh, how do we get out of this one???".

The MYSTERIOUS DARKNESS came right in close over the top of Archie's head and breathed freezing air over him, but before it could turn Archie to ice he quickly pulled the Bluebell emblem off his Parka sleeve and threw it towards Dougie.

"Quick, catch!" said Archie to Dougie.

The emblem turned in to a boomerang and Dougie grabbed it and threw it in to the freezing breath of the MYSTERIOUS DARKNESS shattering it in to tiny icicles that fell to the ground.

"Good work Dougie!!" said Archie.

"Thanks Archie!" said Dougie.

The MYSTERIOUS DARKNESS then grabbed Dougie by his trouser braces and pulled him in to the shadows.

"You think you are clever do you????" said the MYSTERIOUS DARKNESS.

"Aaaaaaaah!" screamed Dougie.

Trevor quickly pulled off his trouser braces made a lasso and he flew on his surf board in to the shadows holding the lasso in one hand and he threw the lasso in to the shadows to grab hold of Dougie.

"Hold on Dougie!" said Trevor.

Archie ZOOMED... straight past Trevor to stop Dougie from reaching the big black hole where he would be lost forever.

Archie just saw Dougie's red hobnail boot sticking out in the shadows and grabbed the end of Trevor's lasso and hooked it round Dougie's ankle.

"Got ya!" said Archie.

"Pull the lasso Trevor" said Archie.

Archie and Trevor pulled and pulled the lasso so hard that Dougie came flying out and fell to the ground.

"Are you ok Dougie?" said Archie.

"Just about…" said Dougie.

The wind was howling again and the MYSTERIOUS DARKNESS started to turn everything in to ice and its icy bony hands could be seen crawling through the woods over everything and up every tree. Icicles were hanging from every branch.

"What now?" said Trevor.

"This!" said Archie.

Archie took off his Parka coat and threw it up above and over Trevor and Dougie to protect them from being frozen by the MYSTERIOUS DARKNESS. The Parka quickly turned in to a huge silver shield GLOWING WITH LIGHT.

"I am Archie descendant of the Zames Robert Clan and I am here to rid YOU the MYSTERIOUS DARKNESS from these woods and planet earth FOREVER!!!!!" said Archie very loudly.

"Trees, you must stand tall and use your branches to push back the wind and the ice and make room for the light.

Bluebells, you must rise from the ground in your glorious colour and reflect your brightness into the darkness.

Bees, you must come out of your hives in your hundreds and thousands and bring with you all the pollen that you have stored" commanded Archie.

There was a FLASH OF LIGHT through the woods!

The trees started to move, the Bluebells started to rise from the ground and the Bees came out from their hives.

Dougie and Trevor flew out from underneath the huge shield to help.

"AAAAAARGGGGH" came a blood-curdling cry from the MYSTERIOUS DARKNESS as it realised that Archie was STRONGER than it thought.

"I WILL NOT LEAVE!!!" screamed the MYSTERIOUS DARKNESS.

"OH YES YOU WILL!!" shouted Archie.

"Bees, Dougie and Trevor on the count of three, you must throw all the pollen into the middle of the woods!" said Archie.

"One, Two, Three!" said Archie.

The Bees, Dougie and Trevor threw all the pollen into the middle of the woods and Archie shouted the MAGIC word "SLLEB-U-ELB!".

The pollen burst into a gigantic ball of light opening up huge holes of light in the darkness. The GOOD LIGHT had emerged!

"WOW, now that's what I call MAGIC!" said Dougie and Trevor.

"GOOD LIGHT! I call upon you to turn the darkness in to light again and destroy the MYSTERIOUS DARKNESS!" said Archie.

"NO!!!!!" screamed the MYSTERIOUS DARKNESS.

"OOPS!... BEHIND YOU!" said the GOOD LIGHT.

"UHH!" said the MYSTERIOUS DARKNESS.

The GOOD LIGHT grabbed the MYSTERIOUS DARKNESS by
its black cloak and pulled it into the light and as it pulled the
MYSTERIOUS DARKNESS in to the light, it pulled all the darkness
out of the sky too.

"AAAAAAARRRGGGGGGH! I WILL NOT GO!!!!!!" screamed the
MYSTERIOUS DARKNESS.

"OH you are GOING!" said the GOOD LIGHT.

GOING, GOING AND GONE!!!!!!!!

At that moment, the MYSTERIOUS DARKNESS disappeared
FOREVER! There was an explosion of light across the woods that
was so strong it knocked Archie, Dougie and Trevor to the ground.

"WOW! We have done it!!!!!" said Archie as he got up.

"Well done Archie!!!" said Trevor and Dougie.

"Look around you!!" said Bob.

"Bob, how did you get back here?" said Archie.

"The minute the GOODLIGHT pulled the MYSTERIOUS DARKNESS in to its light I knew it was safe for me to transport back" said Bob.

"Fantastic result, all of you!!" said Bob.

The light started to shine right through the woods, the trees were standing tall and strong, the ice had melted, the birds were flying around happily, the Bluebells started to bloom smiling in the sunlight.

The Bees were flying busily through the woods carrying the sacks of Bluebell bulbs from BLUEB HQ and releasing them to the ground for more Bluebells to grow. The carpet of Bluebells will once again grow through the entire wood.

"THE WOODS AND PLANET EARTH HAVE BEEN SAVED!!! PHEW!!!" said Archie.

"Thank you Archie, we could never have done this without you and the woods will be eternally grateful to you!" said Dougie and Trevor.

"Sadly, it is time for us to go now" said Dougie.

"Why so soon?!" said Archie.

"Our window in space will disappear and besides, we have to get back to PLANET BLUEB for afternoon tea" said Trevor.

"By the way did you bring the cake?" said Dougie.

"Yes, it's in my rucksack at BLUEB HQ" said Archie.

"Great, we can take that back to enjoy with our afternoon tea!" said Dougie.

"Where's my Parka coat?" said Bob.

"Ah yes, I see I need to turn it back in to one, sorry" said Bob ...and laughed.

Bob clicked his fingers and the huge silver shield that protected Dougie and Trevor from the MYSTERIOUS DARKNESS turned back in to a Parka coat and Bob was wearing it once more.

They all ran back to BLUEB HQ through the beautiful woods.

In they went to BLUEB HQ and Archie gave Dougie the cake and said "How long will it take to you to get home?"

"In the blink of an eyelash" said Trevor.

"WOW!" said Archie.

"Actually….., you have less than two minutes to get back to the lift Archie and Bob, as when we shut the door of BLUEB HQ, the oak tree will open up from the ground to let our spaceship out and the power from the spaceship taking off will be very strong so you must move quickly" said Trevor.

"Ah, it will be a quick goodbye then for now?" said Bob.

"Yes, I think so" said Trevor.

"It was great to meet you and thank you for your help!" said Archie.

"Safe journey home and thank you too" said Bob.

Trevor and Dougie gave Archie a hug, shook Bob's hand and Archie and Bob left BLUEB HQ. The door slammed SHUT!

"QUICK Archie! We need to move!" said Bob.

Archie and Bob ran back to the lift as fast as their legs would carry them, before the MAGICAL DOORWAY to the woods closed FOREVER!

As they got closer to the lift the oak tree opened up and they could feel the strength from the force of the spaceship taking off. Bob pulled the lift door open and jumped in.

"Come on Archie! quick as we have no time left!" said Bob.

Archie took one last look behind him and saw Dougie and Trevor's BLUE SPACESHIP just as it was about to go into the LIGHT.
He jumped into the lift, pulled the door shut pressed the button and they were off!

GONE! Dougie and Trevor were heading home.

DING! The lift was back inside the Grandfather clock and Bob and Archie were exhausted.

They got out of the lift and Bob said the MAGIC word "SLLEB-U-ELB".

Time returned to normal and everything in the house was back in its place as if nothing had ever happened. Bob then clicked his fingers and they were on the landing outside Archie's bedroom.

Archie gave Bob a big hug and said "Will I ever see you again?"

"Who knows????" said Bob.

"By the way, why are Dougie and Trevor called the Bluebs???" said Archie.

"It is all about the Bluebells Archie and as Dougie and Trevor are the keepers of the Bluebell woods in the future, they are called the Bluebells or Bluebs for short. Their planet Blueb is full of Bluebells and they brought the hessian sacks of Bluebells from the future to help replenish what the MYSTERIOUS DARKNESS destroyed" said Bob.

"I understand now, that is amazing!" said Archie.

"Take good care Archie and remember the Bluebell woods will always be here, but we must protect it!" said Bob.

"Thank you and I will" said Archie.

"Ta Ta For Now! or TTFN!" chuckled Bob and then he disappeared into a flash of LIGHT.... GONE!

Archie got into bed, thinking about what he had done that night and smiled with pride and then he was kicking out the zzzZ.

It's morning and the sunlight is streaming through Archie's bedroom window. He got up and looked towards the woods and no longer did it look spooky and sad, but now it looked bright and happy and he could see the striking colour of the carpet of Bluebells trailing through the woods.

Archie went downstairs and the Grandfather clock was not in the hallway!

"Morning Archie" said Aunt Beth from the kitchen.

"Morning" said Archie.

"Where has the Grandfather clock gone?" said Archie.

"Oh that old thing, Mr Augustus came and picked it up this morning as we sold it to him last week. He loves clocks and he said there was something different about this clock and he wanted to add it to his collection. He loved the Bluebells on the clockface" said Aunt Beth.

"That's Bob isn't it! but how can it be as he has gone back in time??" thought Archie.

Archie had just finished breakfast and Uncle Albert came in to the kitchen.

"I've just taken a telephone call from Fiona and their business trip finished earlier than planned, so they are on their way from London now to pick Archie up" said Uncle Albert.

"Time to pack then Archie as they will be here late afternoon" said Aunt Beth.

"I hope you have enjoyed your stay Archie?" said Uncle Albert.

"It has been great, thank you!" said Archie.

Archie packed his suitcase and then spent the rest of the day in the garden with Aunt Beth and Uncle Albert picking more strawberries and gathering vegetables to take back to London with him for his Mum and Dad.

Archie's parents turned up to take him home and they all had afternoon tea together and enjoyed Aunt Beth's wonderful cakes.

It was time to go again and everyone said their goodbyes and Fiona thanked Aunt Beth and Uncle Albert for looking after Archie.

Just as Archie was walking down the hallway to catch up with his Mum and Dad, Aunt Beth gave him a hug and whispered in his ear "thank you for saving the woods Archie" and winked at him.

Archie gasped and said "You know?!" "Yes, Bob told me" said Aunt Beth.

"How, as Bob went back in time?" said Archie.

"Bob does pop in from time to time on his scooter" said Aunt Beth.

"Really?" said Archie.

"Yes and he said you did the Zames Robert Clan proud!" said Aunt Beth.

"You are very welcome" said Archie.

"It is all about the Bluebells Archie, as they are the symbol of everything GOOD to the Zames Robert Clan and that was why the MYSTERIOUS DARKNESS had to be destroyed as it wanted to take everything good away from the woods and the world that we live in past, present and future.

The Bluebs had to come back in time to help as they are part of the future, as are the Bees who keep the Bluebells safe" said Aunt Beth.

"I understand and promise I will Aunt Beth" said Archie.

"You are a STAR!" said Aunt Beth.

Uncle Albert then came over to Archie and said "Please do come back and visit us again next summer".

"Yes, I definitely will!" said Archie.

Archie and his parents drove off back down the gravel drive heading towards the winding lane through the woods, but this time they were driving through a different wood.

It was light, bright and full of beautiful Bluebells as the MYSTERIOUS DARKNESS had gone!

As they came out the other side of the woods Archie turned to look back and for one split second he thought he saw Trevor and Dougie waving goodbye to him, but how could it be them as they had gone home, hadn't they? He looked again and they had gone.

The End!
Or Is It?